The DRAC

THE DRAC

FRENCH TALES OF DRAGONS AND DEMONS
BY FELICE HOLMAN AND NANINE VALEN

DRAWINGS BY STEPHEN WALKER

CHARLES SCRIBNER'S SONS / NEW YORK

J
398.4
H

1 3 5 7 9 11 13 15 17 19 V/C 20 18 16 14 12 10 8 6 4 2
Printed in the United States of America
Library of Congress Catalog Card Number 75-4029
ISBN 0-684-14334-8

CONTENTS

THIS BOOK IS FOR H.V.
WITH L AND K
FROM F AND N

Acknowledgment and thanks for the help of

Mme. R. Zaccarie, librarian, the municipal library of Toulon

M. Louis Janvier, vice president, Society of Friends
of Old Toulon, Archives of Old Toulon

Howard Stambor, doctoral candidate, department of
comparative literature, Yale University

For the courtesies and assistance of the regional
libraries of France, particular thanks to the Paris
Bibliothèque Nationale, and the municipal libraries
of Autun, Besançon, Caen, Dijon, Lons-le-Saunier,
Luçon, Nevers, Niort, Les Sables d'Olonne.

Cherbourg
Valcanville
Barfleur
Montfarville
St. Vaast
Val
de Saire
NORMANDY
Clécy
River Orne
Condé-sur-Noireau

BURGUNDY

FRANCHE
COMTÉ

POITOU

NIVERNAIS

Bourg

BOURBONNAIS

River Rhône

Avignon
PROVENCE
Tarascon
Arles
les Baux
Anti
Draguignan
La Camargue
Îles d'Or

FRANCE

PREFACE

A folktale is just that—a tale *told* by folks. Originally, it was not written or read by folks because there was no good way to do that; there were not many books and very few people who could read. But a good story was told and retold by story-tellers in families and passed down through generations, changed, added to, embroidered, and eventually told to someone who wrote it down in an "oral history" or used it to spin a story of his own. Though the surviving versions vary, the heart of the old tale always beats at the center.

In telling these stories of dragons and demons, we have searched provincial archives, libraries, journals, and attics to find as many versions of a story as possible, and then looked for the basic elements common to all—the heart of the legend. Then we have retold it, keeping the essentials of the regional beliefs and filling in the details that would fall into the traditional storyteller's realm.

All the stories belong to what we call the supernatural, but in France they call them stories of the *fantastique*.

FELICE HOLMAN AND NANINE VALEN

March, 1975

ix

The Drac

THE INVISIBLE DEMON

A dragon of any kind was enough of a terror, but surely the people between Avignon and Arles and down through the Camargue had a dragon more terrible than most because he was often invisible, and though the people of the towns and villages knew this dreadful creature was among them, they could seldom see him. His name was the Drac.

The Drac was more than a dragon; he was a sorcerer, a demon, and an enchanter. He ranged through the swamps of the province but he lived mainly in the river Rhône, and in its very deepest hole he had his household. There in the river some terrified folk might glimpse him occasionally, enormous and lizard-like, naked as a worm, willowy as a lamprey, with two fins of transparent blue lace on his back, webbed feet like the flamingo of the Camargue, and long greenish hair which floated like algae on the waves. For those unlucky enough to be caught by his eyes, they appeared white, glaucous, half-closed, but all-seeing. He was a fury of the waters, and he held the countryside in terror.

But was it not enough that this monster dominated the river in which men sailed and fished and where women did their washing? It was not enough for the Drac. Often disguised as a townsman, and other times completely invisible,

he stalked the marketplace where the villagers came to barter fresh fruit, and game, and fish. The Drac came for his dinner, but he did not come for these foods. He had a taste for human flesh and blood and he would find it in the marketplace, kidnapping some hapless peasant—the younger the better—and no one would see him come and no one would see him go.

But more often he used a ploy that even today makes honest folk cry out in rage. Underneath the river he would lie in wait, showing not even the tip of his tail or a strand of his long green hair above the water. And yet those white eyes saw. They could see the sailors come to walk along the quay, and children come to run or sit on the bank, and the women come to do their washing. And this is how the Drac hunted. If he saw a woman kneeling at the water's edge beating the linen, he would send floating by, almost within her reach, but not quite, a bowl containing a pearl. Pushed forward by greed, the woman would reach out her hand, tempted by the lovely jewel catching the sun. But the bowl would drift away so cleverly that she would lose her balance and fall into the Rhône, and the Drac would catch her, drawing her down in a whirlpool to his home beneath the river.

Or he could capture a child in much the same way, showing him a toy floating on the water. What child could resist the sight of a tiny sailboat fashioned of reeds with a tiny crew of snail shells? Or, if the Drac saw a sailor, he might put a gold coin in the bowl and float it in sight of the young man strolling along the bank. Thus did the Drac keep his larder filled.

One day, a young woman named Jeanne, who had had a child only a few weeks before, came to wash her infant's clothing in the river. She carried her basket balanced on her head with one hand, as did all the other women, and in her other hand she carried a beetle—a wooden paddle used for beating laundry on the rocks. She set her basket on the bank and happily took her new baby's clothes to a rock at the river's edge. And that is when she saw the pearl floating by in the bowl. Quicker than thought she reached, and swifter than her reach the bowl swerved and leaped aside. Losing her balance, her beetle flying from her hand, Jeanne tumbled head first into the Rhône.

The river now blew up a sudden storm. The waves rose, the current quickened, and a whirlpool drew Jeanne down, down, down, in floating flight, through many layers of water until she was deep in the bed of the Rhône river and the very home of the Drac. But the Drac had not captured Jeanne in order to eat her, and as he drew her down through shades of gray, blue, green, and purple into the deepest part of the Rhône, he cast a spell on her wherein her life before this moment became a dream, and her new and well-loved child became a dream, and her husband, Jacques, became a dream. And so, when Jeanne found herself in the lair of the Drac, she was not wild with terror at finding herself there, but only confused as a person awakening from a dream.

When Jeanne had recovered her senses on the sandy floor of the river, the Drac addressed her in his stormy voice, and yet she did not feel afraid.

"Madame," he said, "you have come here to do me a service."

"Oh, indeed, I am at your service, sir," said Jeanne humbly, because she could see that the Drac was some imperial being, and she no longer saw him as the evil creature she had feared all her life.

"I have a child," said the Drac, ". . . a frail and fretful child, and in order to restore him to health it is necessary for him to be nursed by a young human mother such as yourself. This is the only way that he will be able to get the strength he needs."

"Ah, I love children," said Jeanne, "and it will be my pleasure to care for the child of so majestic a person as yourself, sir."

The Drac was pleased with her reply and the Drac-child was brought to Jeanne. He was, indeed, frail and fretful. His color was that of milk glass and his tiny fins were limp and only palely blue. His eyes were entirely closed and there was not a sign of the rich growth of greenish hair that should have shown on his head. He lay limp in the arms of his mother, the Drac-lady, and her white eyes entreated Jeanne to help him. How could Jeanne not help the Drac-child! She held out her arms and took him to her bosom, where only a few hours before her own infant had been, and nursed him. Then she laid the Drac-child in his river bed to sleep.

The Drac had his home in the natural caves on the bottom of the river surrounded by gardens of water plants and shells. For the most part Jeanne kept to the Drac-child's rooms and to the gardens where she and the child took their recreation. But if for any reason she was in the Drac's own rooms and observed him dining on human flesh and blood, opening his white eyes wide and growling as he always did when he ate, she saw him eating not human flesh, but luscious fruits. Then, for example, eyes were cherries, figs were ears, and the human heart was a great purple plum. And this was because of the spell that the Drac had put upon her. For her own diet, the Drac provided roots that were similar to foods she knew, and also the shellfish of the river.

Though the Drac dined on human flesh and blood, he had another important use for the people he captured. He would have his wife compound for him a balm from a little human fat and some river cresses, and this he would rub on his body each time he wished to go into the marketplace to do his hunting. It was this balm that made him invisible. And more than that, the balm was used to rub into the eyes of any Drac-child to give it the Drac power of seeing things that are well hidden to others. So it became one of Jeanne's responsibilities, while she cared for the Drac-child, to treat the child's eyelids each evening with the balm so that as he grew he would, like his father, have the same gift of seeing the invisible.

The Drac gave Jeanne the balm in a case made of scallop shells, and he also gave her a stern warning.

"Each night," he said, "when you have finished using the balm, I command you to wash your hands well in this special water, or something dire will befall you." And he gave Jeanne a pitcher of water upon which he had put a purifying charm. And Jeanne did just as he said—most of the time. But once in a while, at the end of a particularly tiring day with the Drac-child, she forgot to wash her hands and went to sleep with the balm still on her fingers. Then, on awakening to the purple light of the grotto, Jeanne would stretch her arms and, as was her habit, rub her right eye. Before long, because the balm worked more quickly on people, it being human fat, Jeanne acquired the ability to see strange things in the water that had before been invisible to humans. The outer walls of the grotto now appeared shining and crys-

talline and the inner walls covered with silver mirrors. The
sandy floor shone like diamonds, the light in the grotto
turned from purple to bright yellow, and flowers appeared
amid the shells in the gardens. Jewels of enormous size and
unknown names were strewn about like mere rocks, and the
furnishings of the Drac's home seemed fashioned of gold. It
was so beautiful a place that Jeanne did not mourn, when in
her dreams she remembered her home near the banks of the
Rhône. And if she remembered her own child, he did not
seem as real as this Drac-child whom she cared for so ten-
derly.

The Drac-child grew as all children do, almost impercep-
tibly, until one day Jeanne noticed that the child was no
longer an infant. His fins had grown lacy and blue, and his
hair green and full. His eyes, closed when Jeanne first saw
him, now showed white like his father's and his webbed feet
took him swiftly and strongly to any place he wished to go in
the water. Although Jeanne had not been aware of the passing of time, the sand clock showed that seven years had gone
by since the day she had first come to this place.

The Drac-wife, now seeing that her son was grown to an
age where he no longer needed nursing, wished to give his
nursemaid a gift, and she could think of none better than to
send Jeanne back to her very own son whom she had left

seven years before. So the Drac-wife spoke to her husband about it. But the Drac protested.

"That would be unwise, wife," he said. "I have never sent a human back from this house. Although there is a spell on her, who knows how she might betray me in her dreams? A Drac must not let himself be at the mercy of a human."

"Ah, but Jeanne has been loyal and I know that she will always be so," pleaded the Drac-wife. "Let her go to her own child who has been motherless. See how beautifully she has nursed our own fine Drac-child to health."

The Drac relented. One day he cast a second spell and sent Jeanne twirling up through the layers of purple, green, blue, and gray until a whirlpool appeared in the center of the Rhône and in its center spun Jeanne. Then the whirlpool gave a final spin that sent her close to shore and she opened her eyes.

The spell that the Drac had cast upon Jeanne caused everything that had happened in the last seven years to take the form of a dream, and Jeanne emerged from the river as someone waking from sleep. She knelt for a while on the bank in only mild confusion, vaguely looking about for her washbasket and beetle. Then she remembered that her beetle had fallen into the river; but what of her basket? She searched but could not find it and there was no one else at the river's edge to ask. The sun was low. "It must be suppertime," she thought. "I have stayed very long at the river."

On the way home she passed a house that she had never noticed before and wondered how she could have missed so fine and new a house. The small mimosa tree in front of her own door . . . how full it was! Had she been blind not to notice it before? Then she opened her door. There was a bearded man at the hearth, fixing the fire, and a young boy of about seven who looked a great deal like him. In fact, the man looked as if he could be her husband's older brother. Now that was a nuisance! Late for supper, lost her laundry, and now a guest for supper!

The man turned as she opened the door and stared. Then he rose and opened his arms and cried, "Jeanne! Jeanne, my wife! I can hardly believe it! Where have you been these long years? We had despaired of finding you."

Now Jeanne saw that this was, indeed, her husband and she was confused and troubled. And then the child cried, "Mama! Mama!" and came running to her.

Jeanne caught and embraced him but turned, questioningly, to her husband. "I do not understand," she said. "Today I lost my beetle in the river and when I recovered my balance I found my laundry basket had disappeared. Now I have come home and I find that you have grown a beard and my baby is not the three-week-old infant I left in the crib, but a grown child. Tell me what has happened. Have I lost my mind?"

But Jacques did not know what had happened. "We

hunted all over for you and we asked for word of you all around the countryside. Then we had to think that the . . . oh, forgive me, Jeanne. We feared that the Drac had caught you and we despaired!"

Jeanne said, "Ah, I dreamed that once. But he didn't eat me as they say. And I dreamed . . ." But her dream was too vague to recall and it slipped away from her like water through her fingers.

"I think you may have been under some charm or spell," said Jacques. "But now you are home and well and that is all that matters."

That night their neighbors celebrated Jeanne's return with such singing, dancing, and feasting that all the wine in the village was drunk in that single night. The children were allowed to stay up until midnight, too, and they played round games and danced, and ate so many sweet cakes that, for once, they had room for no more. It was a truly happy occasion.

Yet, how quickly life returns to normal. Within a few days Jeanne began again to tend the house, and do the laundry at the river, and go to the market for fruit or fish or just to walk around among the stalls. And then one morning in the marketplace when she was looking at some fresh figs, she saw the Drac standing close by, surveying the scene. Now her dream returned to her quite clearly and she walked over and greeted him.

"Good morning, sir," she said.

The Drac was surprised that anyone would speak to him when he knew himself to be much hated and feared and also invisible. But when he saw who it was that had spoken to him he became very very wary and suspicious.

"Good morning, Madame," he said, looking very closely at Jeanne with his white eyes.

But Jeanne was not alarmed. "And how is your family, sir?" she asked, now able, in his presence, to remember clearly the Drac-child and the Drac-wife from her dream.

"Well, thank you, Madame. And yours?"

"Ah, quite beautiful, sir. My son is now grown like your own."

Meanwhile, the people in the market, hearing Jeanne mumbling to what seemed to be empty air, agreed among themselves that she was addled, no doubt, from those empty seven years for which she could say nothing.

Now the Drac looked straight into Jeanne's eyes and asked, "What do you see when you see me?"

"Why, sir, I see you as you are," said Jeanne.

The Drac reached out and covered Jeanne's left eye with one of his fins. "Do you see me now?" he asked.

"Why yes, sir."

Then the Drac took away the fin and covered her right eye instead.

"And do you see me now?" he asked.

"Why no, sir. No. What has happened?"

"Nothing that cannot be undone," the Drac growled, because now he realized that Jeanne had acquired the power in her right eye to see things that are invisible to other humans, and he was furious. He growled again in the way he did when he was about to eat. But he remembered, too, that his wife had wished Jeanne to stay with her own child and so he curbed his impulse to snatch her up and carry her off or devour her on the spot.

"Woman!" he thundered, and Jeanne shuddered. She had never seen him so terrible. "Did you not wash your hands in the special water whenever you used the balm on the eyes of my son?"

"Yes sir, I did," she said. "Almost all the time."

"*Almost* all the time!" the Drac fumed furiously. "And now you have the power to see the invisible and can tell your countrymen when the Drac is among them. Can you not?" And he opened his white eyes wide again and Jeanne felt a chill of fear.

"I suppose I could, sir, but . . ."

"And would you not?"

"No! No, I would not, sir, because your wife was most kind to me and because of the Drac-child."

"Not even though you are now here among your own people who may fall under my hand? What if, in some disguise, I were near your very own child, Madame?"

Jeanne shuddered. "Oh, no!" she cried. "No!"

"Wouldn't you then point to me and say, 'Oh, there is the Drac!' " And his white eyes flashed and Jeanne wept because she knew that she would.

And as Jeanne cried, she put her hands over her face, and while her face was hidden, the Drac raised his great blue fins and cast another spell upon her so that, when she took her hands from her face, she had entirely lost the sight in her right eye and with it her ability to see the Drac. Jeanne cried out in fright and horror and ran home weeping to tell the fearful story to her husband and child.

In the years that followed, Jeanne told the story many times, and other people told it too, but no vision ever returned to her right eye, and she never wished it to because of what she might see. She lived quietly and happily with her husband and child, and when she did her washing she kept a tight hold on the beetle and did not covet anything that passed by in the river.

A FEW WORDS ABOUT THE STORY OF
THE DRAC

This is what is surely known about the Drac: that in Gaelic
drak means dragon; that the Provençal town of Draguignan
(originally called Draconeum) is said to owe its name to this
creature who lured many to their deaths in the waters where
he made his home.

A number of people have written about the Drac and the
stories vary. The French poet Mistral wrote his "Poème du
Rhône" in the nineteenth century, but he based it on a much
older Latin work by Gervais of Tilbury, written in the early
thirteenth century. In this collection of legends and supersti-
tions called *Otia imperialia,* Tilbury described the *dracae* as
female aquatic spirits who lured people to their lairs by *taking the form* of the cup that floated by. We have based our
story on Tilbury's, which contains the essential elements—
the washerwoman, the underwater lair, the nursing of the
Drac child, the fat that allowed the woman to see the invisible Drac. However, our Drac is male as it is in many other
accounts.

It is said that the Dracs continued to haunt the provinces
until the fifth century when St. Hermentaire was made
Bishop of Antibes. Today in the region of the Rhône many

washerwomen still use beetles sculpted in the lizard-like shape of the Drac.

BIBLIOGRAPHY

Bérenger-Féraud, L. J. B. *Contes populaires des Provençaux de l'Antiquité et du Moyen Age.* Paris: Ernest Leroux, 1887.

————. *Les Légendes de la Provence.* Paris: Ernest Leroux, 1888.

Mistral, Frédéric. *Le Poème du Rhône* (12 Chants). Paris: Alphonse Lemerre, 1897. French trans. from Provençal.

Guide de la Provence mystérieuse, Les Guides Noirs. Paris: Tchou, 1965.

The DEVIL'S FIELD

THE CARPENTER'S CROP

In Clécy there is a very large field and in its exact center is the tallest and oldest elm tree in Normandy. For as long as anyone can remember, a very tall man—perhaps twenty feet tall—has been seen pacing around the tree at night. He walks and walks incessantly. As the years pass, his costume changes because he is a gentleman of fashion. At one time, for example, he had worn a tailcoat and a large tie. Much earlier he was seen in a black outfit of short kneepants, buckled shoes, and a sword at his side. Only a short while ago he was dressed like any other man of the time. But however he dresses he always carries a large rake on his shoulder, and should any person or animal pass within reach, he will find himself scratched and scraped by the sharp teeth of the rake, and he will not likely go that close again.

Sometimes the tall man leaves in his place a large white greyhound who lies quietly beneath the elm. And if some townsman, coming home from an evening's amusement in the village, takes a shortcut through this field, he might see the greyhound stand and grow until it is as big as a horse. Then, the huge greyhound has been known to either jump on the back of the late walker or push him on his way, following at his heels so closely that the great dog's breath burns the man's ears. The dreadful persistent beast may stay with the man until he has gone through the door of his own house, where he will no doubt be scolded by his wife for missing supper.

Though the very tall man who paces around the elm tree looks like a gentleman, it is known by all who he truly is and the place is called the Devil's Field, and the devil's field it is.

On one particular evening, a very poor carpenter, named Evariste, had lingered too long in the tavern at Condé-sur-Noireau, and it was very late when he started for home. He knew that he had missed his supper and that his wife would be furious at his spending the little he earned. He should have hurried but he did not like walking alone at night, with the shriek of the night birds and the strange touch of unknown things. So he hurried no more than a crayfish, looking over his shoulder from time to time, and thinking that perhaps, after all, he should have stayed for another glass of wine just to give him courage.

As Evariste approached the Devil's Field the sound of the birds seemed to cease and the air was still and strange. The bushes brushing against him felt like hands and he frequently jumped back and away from them. Then he heard something snap and fall on his foot and he found with horror that he could not lift his foot from the ground. When he had the courage to bend over and feel what great force pinned him to the place, he discovered it was only a twig which he lifted from his foot with two fingers. Though his foot was easily freed from its mysterious trap, he moved on with ever-increasing fear.

Now, this carpenter was no weakling. He was six feet tall and strong enough to lift a cow, and yet, when suddenly he saw a tall man in a black overcoat approaching him, he cringed and could have been pushed over by an angry child. As the man came closer, Evariste could see that he wore a black felt hat with a bright red feather in it, and this bright feather was lit by the moonlight and blew in the night wind.

"Good evening, carpenter," said the man.

The carpenter, hearing himself greeted in this manner, quivered as if he had been bitten by a snake and did not answer.

"You seem frightened," said the man.

"I am, sir," replied Evariste, who was a truthful man. "It is known that the devil, himself, frequents this field."

The man laughed and his laugh gave him away because the carpenter, though he had never heard the devil laugh, recognized the sound instantly.

"But you *are* he, are you not?" And Evariste turned to run.

The man laughed again. "You've guessed it, carpenter. But do not run away. Perhaps you will find I am not so evil.

Come sit with me on this log and let us talk. It may be to your profit."

Something compelled Evariste to turn and join the devil who now had seated himself on a log in the moonlight at the edge of the enormous field.

"I think," the devil said, "that luck has not visited your house lately. Am I right?"

"Oh," said Evariste sadly, "I am a most unlucky man. I can grow a pear tree and it will bear pears, and an apple tree which will bear apples, but I have not had any luck in making money grow."

"And you have children," said the devil pleasantly, as if conducting a conversation in a tavern with a friend.

"I have eight," said the carpenter. "Lazy, every one of them, and believe me when I tell you that it is hard to feed them all."

"A sad story," said the devil. "How much do you earn?"

"Nearly nothing," said Evariste.

The devil laughed. "And even that nothing you spend in the tavern on wine."

The carpenter shrugged. "Well, a little wine now and then . . ." But it frightened him that this devil knew so much about him.

"I think we can do some business together," said the devil.

"I know nothing of business," Evariste said. "Nothing at all."

"I'll teach you," the devil said, "and if you learn your lesson well, I will make you a rich man."

"In that case," said Evariste, "I would be a willing student."

"Good," the devil said. "Right now, you will go home . . ."

"My wife . . . she's going to be standing at the door with a bucket of water!" Evariste now remembered that he was later than ever because he had stopped to talk with the devil. He had no idea how much time had passed.

"Think of the riches that await you and you'll be able to bear it," said the devil.

"But surely I will not get rich simply by going home," Evariste said.

"That is true. But in the morning you will go out and buy this field from its owner."

"Buy this field! I? And with what, pray?"

The devil threw the carpenter a leather purse. "With that. Do you know the owner?"

"I know of him. Old Harpagon. Everyone does. He's a lender of money for which he milks his clients of huge amounts of interest. That's why he's so rich."

"Ah, yes," said the devil. "A thief and a scoundrel. He'll do anything for gold. But you must tell him only that you are buying his property to farm it."

"Farm this! The devil's own field!" And then the carpenter

was afraid that his remark may have angered the devil. "I beg your pardon, sir," he said nervously.

"Don't be alarmed. My feelings are not delicate. But don't forget; not a word to old Harpagon about the true reason you are buying the field. That's one part of the agreement."

"One part," said Evariste. "What is the other, then?"

"We'll talk of that when we meet again tomorrow night at this very spot. Then you will return with the deed to the property and a shovel."

"A shovel?"

"Tomorrow night with a shovel and the deed." With that, the devil walked away, and as he approached the great elm, he disappeared.

The carpenter arose from the log and was alarmed to find that while it was not yet midnight when he arrived here, a rooster was crowing now and the light of the sun was beginning to show. He wondered if he had dreamed this whole thing, fallen sleep, perhaps, on the long walk home. But then he felt the bag of coins in his pocket, and before him he saw the devil's footsteps in the soft earth of the path. And then an astounding thing happened. As the light of the sun hit the path, every place that the devil had put his right foot a clump of garlic now sprang up, and wherever he had put his left foot a clump of onion grew. And if the carpenter had any doubt about his companion of the night, he had none now.

Evariste continued his journey home knowing what kind of reception he would get. He guessed correctly. His wife had fallen asleep in her chair and the fire was out. As he opened the door, she awakened crying, "Where have you been? You frightened us to death. Were you in the tavern all night? Where have you been? Where have you been?"

And the carpenter told the truth as was his habit. "I've been in the Devil's Field talking to the devil, that's where I've been."

"Do you think I have no wits at all!" his wife exclaimed. "Talking to the devil, indeed! And what could he have said to you, you foolish man!"

The carpenter was silent. It was bad enough that his wife was angry and worried about his late arrival home, but here *he* was the innocent victim of an awesome meeting with the devil, and all he got was a tongue-lashing and mistrust. Evariste found himself getting very angry and, turning on his heel, he stamped out and slammed the door.

It now being morning, he decided to find the house of Harpagon which was on the north side of the town. He crossed the Orne river and took a footpath that led up the side of the valley on the right bank of the stream. There he found the shabby house of the rich but stingy man. The carpenter knocked at the door. No answer. He knocked again, and then again until a very rumpled-looking Harpagon appeared at a window above.

"Who is that at this hour of the morning?" Harpagon shouted.

"It is Evariste, the carpenter. I'm sorry to disturb you, sir, but most townspeople are up at this hour."

"Well, Harpagon is not most townspeople. What do you want? To borrow money, of course."

"Not at all. I want to give you money," said Evariste.

"Give me money? A debtor are you? I'll be right down."

But when old Harpagon had come downstairs in his nightshirt and the carpenter had explained that he had not come to repay money, since he owed none, but to buy the field, Harpagon did not believe him.

"Field? Field? What field can you mean?"

"The big field on the other side of the crossroads on the road to Condé-sur-Noireau," said Evariste. "I have the money to pay for it. I want to farm it." And when he said that he cringed a bit because he did not usually lie.

"Farm *that* field! The field that . . ." and Harpagon did not finish his remark. "Well, you couldn't afford my price, anyway."

Evariste threw down the purse and pushed it toward Harpagon. Harpagon's love of gold moved his hands toward the purse and he opened it and counted the pieces. "Twenty-five thousand francs!" he exclaimed. Now Harpagon was amazed, but he did not forget he was a businessman.

"Well," he said. "Perhaps, after all, I will sell you the field. But I will write in the deed that you may not farm it until I die."

Evariste looked doubtful. But Harpagon said, "That won't be long. I'm an old man. Look at me." So Evariste thought that perhaps this would satisfy the devil. He had said only to bring the deed. He had said nothing of conditions.

"Sold!" said Evariste, and he received the deed to the infamous field of the devil.

The carpenter spent the rest of the day walking around the countryside until it should be time for his meeting with the devil. When he left Harpagon's house, he crossed over to the left bank of the stream, into a meadow, and keeping to the edge of the woods, he came to a path that rose quickly to a hillock called the Sugarloaf. From here he could view the whole sweep of the river Orne. He sat there half the day pondering the interesting turn of his life which was like the turn of the river, and he could not help wondering where the river flowed.

At nightfall he returned to the tavern and emptied a bottle of wine with a friend from whom he borrowed a shovel. Then he set out for the Devil's Field. The devil was there before him waiting on the log.

"Good! You keep your appointments. I'm glad to see that.

That's a good start for our business together," the devil said.

The carpenter was pleased with the praise. He thought this devil was not so bad a fellow as it was said. "Here's the deed, sir. There's just this one thing. Harpagon says I am not to farm the field until the day he dies."

"And you shall not," said the devil. "If you should want to plant anything after tonight, you will wait for his death. Now let's get to work. Bring your shovel."

The devil led the carpenter into the field and Evariste was surprised to find that the ground of the field felt just like any field—quite solid under his feet—and the only notable thing was the strong odor of onion and garlic.

"Now just here," said the devil, stopping in front of a particular pear tree in a long line of pear trees, "you will begin to dig."

And with no hint of what he was doing, the carpenter began to dig. After quite a lot of hard digging he hit something that clanked against his shovel. He dug carefully around the object and uncovered a barrel.

"Bring it up," said the devil.

The carpenter tried to lift it, but though he was as strong a man as there was in Clécy, he could not budge the barrel alone. However, using the shovel for a lever and with the help of the devil, himself, he managed, puffing and sweating, to raise it from the hole.

"Open it," commanded the devil. And the carpenter, using the shovel blade, pried off the top. Gold sprang from the barrel like carp from a pool.

"Half of that is yours," said the devil, and he whipped out a parchment and a pen, and held them toward the befuddled and reeling Evariste. "Just sign this receipt and document of agreement."

"What does it say?" asked the carpenter.

"Oh, just the usual formalities," the devil answered. "It states that, in return for the gold and the field, you will transfer possession of your soul to me at the time of your death."

"My soul! My death!" cried Evariste.

"Correct. Just sign here." And seeing the carpenter draw back and hesitate, the devil said, "Unless, of course, you prefer to forget the arrangement and leave the field and the gold . . ."

Evariste looked at the gold overflowing the barrel in the moonlight, and he took the pen and signed the parchment. But he said to himself, "My death is many years away. In that time I will think of a way out of this. I'm sure of that."

The devil smiled with satisfaction. Quickly, he took a sack from under his coat and piled half the gold in the sack, leaving half in the barrel for the carpenter. Then he said, "Do what you like with your share. The field will be yours to farm, if you wish, when Harpagon dies. Live well, and good-by until we meet once more." And he was gone.

The carpenter stood regarding his treasure and considered what to do with it. And as he stood there, the white grey-hound appeared near the great elm tree in the middle of the field and lay down. He did not seem to notice Evariste who had now come to a decision. He took a few pieces of gold from the barrel and put them in his pocket. Then, with great effort, he rolled the barrel into the hole again and filled it with earth. Over this he put pieces of grassy sod, and when he was through, no one would have known that the place had been disturbed. But Evariste noted the place well. He had waited a long time to be rich and he could wait a little longer.

When the carpenter arrived home his wife began to scold again, but he silenced her by dropping a goldpiece on the table in front of her. It sweetened her tongue as if it were a drop of honey from a honeycomb.

In two months' time Harpagon was dead and, sad to say, he was not much missed except that now there was no one in Clécy to lend money. But now that Evariste possessed the field, free and clear, and could do as he wished, he began to think there might be something more profitable for him than farming. He decided that if he were to plant anything at all in that field it would not be beans. And so he became a money-lender in Harpagon's place. He dug up his half-barrel of gold and lent half of it at a very high interest and before long the half-barrel became a full barrel again. And then he took half of that and lent it at very high interest and it became another barrel full of gold which he buried in the ground near the first. And each time that he had to build another barrel to hold the gold he sang very cheerfully because he had thought of a very very clever plan.

Despite his new wealth the carpenter continued to live in his shabby house and did not use the gold to make a more comfortable life for himself or for his wife or his eight children. And then, before long, he was not so welcome in the tavern among his former friends who now considered him a greedy person and a mean one, too. At first this surprised Evariste, but he got used to being alone and soon he began to prefer it, as barrel after barrel of gold found its way into the ground around the pear tree and the years went by. He even had a sort of fame. Now everyone knew him as Evariste, the money-lender, not Evariste, the carpenter.

Evariste's children were now grown and one after another they had left Clécy to marry or to make a living in another province. And Evariste's wife grew old and finally died, leaving him quite alone in his old age. But he did not feel lonely very often, being constantly busy dealing in money, digging up barrels by the light of the moon when no one would see him, and building and burying new ones. He carefully paced off their positions in the ground around the pear tree, and many times he could see the white greyhound, paying no attention, lying beneath the great elm. And one day Evariste noticed that a young pear tree had sprung up some yards from where he stood.

"I've never noticed that one," he said. "Another tree for the orchard. Gold is not all that grows here."

And then one morning when Evariste had been feeling like quite an old man, a very young man came to the house.

"Good day, sir," the young man said.

"Not so good when you are old," said Evariste. And, indeed, his back was quite crippled now from the digging and lifting of barrels.

"My name is Paul La Chance, and I have come to make an offer that should cheer you," said the young man.

"And what would that be?" asked Evariste.

"I will buy your field on the road to Condé-sur-Noireau, and I will pay you fifty thousand francs for it."

"Fifty thousand francs! For the field that . . . for the field on the road to Condé-sur-Noireau!" And Evariste thought that was an offer too great to resist because he, himself, had paid only twenty-five thousand for it. Still, there was a problem—the gold was in the field. On the other hand, fifty thousand francs was a lot of gold to add to his hoard and aid in his clever plan. And then he remembered how he had bought the field from old Harpagon. He said to La Chance, "In return for the fifty-thousand francs I will give you a deed which will make you owner of the field, free and clear, upon my death." The young man hesitated, so Evariste hurried on. "In fact, I will throw in this house, too. You will be my heir. How's that!"

"That's a bargain," said La Chance, and they signed the deed.

It was only a couple of months after that that Evariste was taken quite ill and was very near to dying. But he had planned his whole life around this moment and he was sure he had planned it well so he was not alarmed. Nevertheless, he was surprised when he awakened one night to find the great white greyhound standing beside his bed. He drew back under his covers but the mastiff pushed him out of bed with his nose, and then pushing and nudging, he headed Evariste down the stairs, out the door, and through the empty streets of Clécy at a great pace. Evariste did not think that at his age and in his weakened health he could move so fast, but he did. He fairly flew, with the great dog behind him, past the crossroads, onto the road to Condé-sur-Noireau, and straight to the Devil's Field.

Suddenly the greyhound ceased pushing and disappeared. Evariste sat down on the grass to catch his breath. And then, from behind the great elm, the devil, himself, appeared. He approached swiftly and smiled pleasantly.

"We meet again," he said.

"We do," said Evariste, shivering a bit in the chill breeze.

"I just want to remind you of our agreement," said the devil, whipping out the old parchment and looking, Evariste thought, a bit sly. But sly or not, old Evariste thought he, himself, was the slyer of the two.

"I think, sir," said Evariste, "that you will find it to your advantage to tear up that agreement. I have something much better to offer you."

"Indeed?" asked the devil.

"Indeed, yes. Now you will hear how I have devoted my life to your interest." Evariste leaned forward eagerly. "I did not lie when I told old Harpagon that I would use his field to farm."

"A farmer, are you?" asked the devil.

"Ah, such a farmer!" cried Evariste, grabbing the devil's arm. "I have been planting gold. Gold! And now that mere half-barrel that you gave me all those years ago has grown to a crop of thirty barrels. Thirty barrels of gold! And it's yours . . . all yours!" He sat back to see the effect on the devil.

The devil looked serious. "Do you mean you are offering to buy your soul for thirty barrels of gold?"

"No, no! I am simply offering you a gift of something finer than my soul." But for the first time Evariste felt some doubts.

Suddenly the devil threw back his head and laughed, and it was the laugh that Evariste had heard and recognized that first night when they had met in the dark field. He laughed for a long time, and as he did, Evariste felt cold and frightened.

"Carpenter," the devil said, when he had stopped laughing. "What is valuable to one may not be so valuable to another. Some, for example, collect gold. And I, for example, collect souls." The devil put his face close to Evariste's and whispered, "Now, if it *were* gold I wished for . . ."

"Yes, yes? If it *were* gold you wished for . . ."

"If it were gold I wished for," and the devil laughed again, *"there are barrels of gold under every tree in this field!* Let us go."

The next day Paul La Chance moved into the carpenter's house.

A FEW WORDS ABOUT THE STORY OF
THE DEVIL'S FIELD

This story is based on a version of the same name by V.-A. Brunet as it appeared in a journal in Normandy in the year 1869. In Brunet's account of the local legend, the carpenter does not replace old Harpagon as the village money-lender. Instead he was said to have promised to stop drinking. But Brunet, himself, found this difficult to believe since he knew the local love of wine, and he quotes the old French proverb, "he who has drunk will drink." In his version it is not known whether or not, at the death of the carpenter, Satan insisted on fulfilling the bargain.

The white greyhound which lies under the elm *does* feature in Brunet's story and is a typical example of what is called a *galipote*. A *galipote* is a nocturnal animal most often seen in the West of France—in the old province of Poitou—and farther north in Normandy. It may more commonly take the form of a white sheep, a bearded goat, a black dog, or even a pig, and may often be seen prowling around farms attacking watchdogs.

Most often, however, the *galipote* frightens the late-night traveler, jumping on his back and urging him home, as he does in this story. Sometimes he is considered as an animal transformed from human by sorcerer's powers. Or, as in this story, he may be a demon in another guise.

BIBLIOGRAPHY

Brunet, V.-A. *Légendes Normandes.* "Le Champ du Diable," from the *Journal de Mortain,* 24 Nov. 1869, #47.

Guillemet, Gaston. *Au Pays vendéen.* Niort: G. Clouzot, 1906.

The Tarasque

THE TERROR OF NERLUC

The wildest of winds, the mistral, tears through southern France like many lashes of a whip. It cuts down trees, rocks houses, and pours the sea and rivers up over the land. For days at a time it rules the provinces and every human or animal—the strongest man and the smallest ant—seeks the cover of house or hole. That is when the old women known for magic powers used to take the cream pot hooks from their hearths and throw them at the sky. This was said to cause violent storms to cease. But in the case of the mistral it was a useless act. At its fiercest nothing could stop it, and on the high cliffs of Les Baux nothing could stand up to it. Nothing but one creature—the Tarasque.

The ferocity of the mistral was nothing compared to that of this dragon. His size was enormous, defying description. His body looked most like an ox but with six short bear-like legs with enormous claws. On his body he had two shields like those of a turtle but covered with curved spikes, and the rest of his body was covered with closely overlapping scales that formed his armor. His tail was long and curved like a scorpion. His head was that of a lion, yet with a horse's ears, but his face, with eyebrows and mustache, was that of a sad and bitter old man. From his nostrils poured smoke and from a distance his breath could make a man faint. His burning dung caused fields to burst into flames, and anything that fell beneath his terrible claws was torn to tinder.

While the Tarasque roamed the pastures, ravaged the fields, and destroyed the herds, it was thought that the creature was both leviathan and behemoth—a creature of water and land—and that he lived beneath a rock in the river which now supports the ruins of the castle of King René. Strong currents prevented anyone from approaching the spot, but one could see the sudden, violent surge of water as the beast prepared to rise from his lair to roam and forage. Where his feet fell, the earth became bare. When he walked across the land, his scales made a thunderous sound that announced his approach, and from a distance one could see flashes of bright light.

When some particularly dreadful thing had happened—if some child had disappeared or a shepherd had been gobbled down with his flock—the people of Nerluc would gather and discuss some new way to try and rout the terrible Tarasque. There was one year, for example, when the dragon seemed to spend much of his time in the water near the big rock, and when he lashed his tail at that place, the river flooded its banks and small boats downstream capsized and sank. That year it was decided to send sixteen of the finest soldiers, in heavy armor and carrying the strongest and sharpest spears, to find and kill the Tarasque. The soldiers moved silently at night, hoping to surprise the monster when he rose from the river and came through the marsh. They camped close to the rock beneath which the Tarasque was thought to dwell. Fifteen men went to sleep so that they might be strong in the morning for the fight, and one was placed on guard.

They had been sleeping only one hour when the guard awoke them saying, "Look comrades, the sun is rising. We had best be alert."

"How can the sun be rising? We've scarcely put our heads down," said one.

"Perhaps it has been a very short night," said a second.

But a third soldier was more observant. "It is odd," he said, "that the sun rises so soon and also that it rises in the *west*."

Then, from the place where the light showed, came the dreadful thundering footsteps of the Tarasque, and before they had more than time to realize that the light was not that of the sun but rather the fires of the dragon himself, out for some midnight marauding, the Tarasque was upon them. He devoured eight of the soldiers, and the eight others, mauled and out of their minds, returned to the city and never said a sensible thing again.

And so another year would pass until the people were able to muster their courage and consider yet another way to bring down their tormenter. When it was still thought that spears would be the best way to conquer the creature—that there must be some place on the Tarasque's armored body that could be penetrated by good steel—every man in the city was set to tempering and honing metal until it was so sharp it could slice a leaf into two leaves, but so strong it could pierce a chestnut beam. When a hundred spears had been sharpened, they were taken into the deep forest that separated the city and pastures from the swamp. Then each spear was fixed to a tree on either side of a long avenue of elms, so that the Tarasque, in passing, would be attacked and skewered by fifty spears on one side and fifty spears on the other, each held by a strong tree. And should the monster go backward or forward, he would be surrounded by spears, and surely one would find a chink in his armor.

The people then retreated a distance to await the Tarasque who was known to use this path to the pasture lands. He did not come the first day and he did not come the second. But on the third day, just as some of the people were about to give up and return home, the great dragon appeared on the crest of the hill. The sound of his step was heard and his fires were seen, and as he approached he appeared so enormous that many onlookers took fright and ran. But those who stayed saw a sight that was never entirely believed by those who did not see it. Moving at a fast pace, the Tarasque charged into the woods and toward the avenue of trees, and when his body had passed through that place, each spear was bent like the breastbone of a guinea fowl, and each spear tip was as blunt as a hammer head. And the Tarasque? He moved on into the pasture unscathed.

And still another time, a famous fighter named Étienne Roland devised twelve catapults, using the tallest and most flexible poplar trees. These catapults were mounted on a hillock overlooking the pasture where the Tarasque hunted. Boulders so large that they must be lifted by six men were made ready for the catapults to fling when Roland would give the signal. It was thought that even if the boulders did not kill the Tarasque outright—and there was that fear—he would most certainly be buried on the spot by the sheer weight of the onslaught, and his tomb would be built by the stones themselves as they fell one upon the other.

When the Tarasque was in full view below them and Roland gave the signal, even the men manning the catapults doubted what they saw and heard. The boulders flew through the air exactly as Roland had said they would, and they fell exactly in the spot Roland had chosen. But as each boulder struck the armor of the Tarasque, the thunderous noise was so great that it was said crockery in the city itself was broken by the din, and the men on the hillock were deafened for life. And the Tarasque? He flicked off the boulders as if they were blue flies, and continued through the pastures where he devoured a herd of choice sheep.

And another year passed.

Among the haunts known to be favored by the Tarasque were the great masses of rock of Les Baux, which rose suddenly from the flat plains like enormous stony hands thrust from the earth. The sides of these cliffs were as sheer and straight as those of a house wall, and an idea occurred to one of the city fathers of Nerluc when he passed there one day, hurrying his donkey so that he might be home by dark.

"Let us admit the obvious," he told the people. "The Tarasque has superior strength and we will never conquer him with might. But let us use our superior human wits against those of this creature."

And then he told them his plan, which was to build a false edge to one of the cliffs of Les Baux—an edge that would *look* secure, but would in reality be flimsy. His idea was to lure the Tarasque to it, and arrange it so that when he stepped upon the false edge, he would fly through space and fall to a gory death on the rocks below.

To carry out this plan, young saplings were hauled up the path on the north side of the rock face, and these were used to build a light platform, which was then suspended by strong ropes over the edge of the south cliff, just even with the top surface. Then the saplings were covered with a sprinkling of small stones and a few tufts of dried grass and wild thyme, which were to make it look as if it were a part of the real cliff. When this was ready and declared the perfect trap, a freshly killed hare was used to lay a trail of blood along the path, and then the hare itself was thrown onto the platform.

The workers now withdrew to one of the many caves of Les Baux from which they could see their ingenious device snare the terrible Tarasque. This time the dragon obliged them by arriving quickly. Perhaps he had come there for the mere pleasure of the place or to survey the lands below, because there was little to be hunted here on the barren rock except red lizards and green beetles, which would be less to him than one grain of salt might be to a man. As was expected the Tarasque found the trail of blood, and following it, arrived at the edge of the cliff where he could see the hare, which surely was not more than enough to stick in a tooth.

Then things happened so quickly that it takes longer to tell about it. The Tarasque put one of his six enormous feet on the false edge, and at the touch of it, the entire contraption—saplings, rocks, grasses, and hare—went flying over the cliff, leaving only a few ropes swinging in the wind. And the Tarasque, only a little irritated at losing so small a bite, stood on the edge of the cliff, as if cast in bronze, surveying the land toward the sea. He stood there so long, in fact, that the people in the cave missed two days of meals and nearly froze when the cold night fell and the wind rose. On the third day the Tarasque went down to the plain to hunt again, and the people went back to Nerluc, defeated and discouraged.

And then one day of one year, there came drifting to the shores near the Islands of Gold, a small boat without oars or sail or rudder, which sailed simply at the will of the wind and the water. The boat carried a young woman named Martha, who with her sisters and her servant Marcelle, had been cast adrift in Syria seven days before. It was so delicate a craft that when a wave finally cast it onto the land, it fell apart like so many sticks.

After they had rested for the night, these sea travelers separated and went different ways through the countryside to speak to the pagan people who did not know of God. Martha and Marcelle chose the path up the valley of the Rhône, through woods and fields, talking to people along the way and doing kind and good things. Word of this young girl and her quiet, good work reached the town of Nerluc before her, so that when she arrived there she was made very welcome. It was not long before the people began to tell her about the Tarasque and its dreadful deeds, and of their constant fear. But none of those who spoke to her could have imagined what she then did. In her simple white dress, and wearing no shield and carrying no sword, Martha walked alone and barefoot, out of the city, across the meadows and woods and marsh in search of the Tarasque. Back in Nerluc the people wrung their hands and cried out that this lovely young girl was going to her death. But Marcelle, who had stayed behind at Martha's request, told them to have faith.

As Martha crossed the marsh, the burning footsteps of the Tarasque were clear before her. As she reached a rise in the land she was able to see him some distance ahead, devouring a sheep, and as he thrashed about, the ground quivered. Martha did not stop. Her white dress blowing in the breeze soon caught the eye of the Tarasque who, seeing her, reared up and threw open his still bloody mouth to roar at the pleasure of another morsel to appease his appetite.

And yet, instead of turning to flee as had all the other victims, Martha continued her steady approach until she was only a few lengths from the monster. Now the Tarasque drew back on his hind legs and began to lunge. At that moment Martha knelt, and taking two sticks from the ground, she formed a cross and held it high above her head before the strange face of the Tarasque. The effect was as if the dragon had been run through with a sword. He stood frozen in his position, his eyes glazed, his muscles paralyzed. Then Martha untied a small jar of holy water from her belt and sprinkled it

on the creature, and all the fires that burned in him were quenched with just a few drops.

Now Martha approached so close that the breath of the Tarasque should have burned her. She knelt again, this time in front of his open mouth. She took her long braids of dark hair, and using one of the sword-like teeth of the dragon as a knife blade, she cut off her braids. These she tied together and laid over the neck of the monster as a bridle, and then she led him, mild as a lamb, back across the swamp, through the woods, across the meadows, and through the gates of the city.

When the sentries on the turret of the gate saw her coming, one thought it was the result of a wish and the other thought it was a trick of the sun, and so neither said anything for fear of being thought ridiculous. And so, Martha, unheralded, appeared in the main square with the Tarasque on a leash.

When the people saw her they were happy and thankful, but they were still fearful and vengeful, too. As Martha stood with the enormous, docile creature, who only a while before and for so many years had been an unspeakable terror, each person raised a sword, a spear, a stick, or a rock, and threw it at the Tarasque. One single stone could have done the work, for now this monster was as vulnerable as any. He fell slowly to his six knees and then collapsed, his great lion's head with its sad old man's face falling to the stones. And Martha cried because she could not bear brutality to any person or animal, but she forgave the people because she understood their long suffering.

After that, the city of Nerluc changed its name to Tarascon, and the official seal bore the image of the dread dragon. Even today a plaster effigy of the Tarasque is paraded twice a year in festivals. Inside, there are eight men, for the eight men who were devoured when the soldiers went to fight him. The men inside the great plaster Tarasque work the machinery and cause the monster to lunge, to roar, to frighten the crowd that comes to watch.

And then a little girl, dressed as Martha, emerges from the crowd and approaches the Tarasque to subdue him . . . until next year.

A FEW WORDS ABOUT THE STORY OF

THE TARASQUE

Unwinding the story of the Tarasque is like unraveling a big ball of twine. Near the center of the ball is the myth of Hercules, conqueror of the Provençal monster *Tauriscus*. Further along is the history of Martha, the prophetess. She was a different Martha than the one in our story, however, who was St. Martha of Bethany, sister to Mary and Lazarus. The first Martha was a Syrian who accompanied the Roman general Marius, defender of Provence from the northern barbarians. In modern legend it is St. Martha who emerged as the savior of the region and the heroine of the story, leaving the Syrian Martha and Hercules behind in dusty and often forgotten books.

It is possible, too, that at the beginning of our present geological period, the people of the region had to fight some survivor of the prehistoric reptiles, or the ancestors of a breed of wild bulls that still roam the swamps of the Camargue.

The earliest description of the monster was written in the ninth century by Raban Maur, archbishop of Mayence, who wrote the first biography of St. Martha. There is a later account by St. Marcel who described the Tarasque in much the way we have. Our description is based, however, on a thir-

teenth-century description by Gervais of Tilbury, a gentleman of Arles. According to him the Tarasque was the land
monster of the lower Rhône, just as the Drac was the aquatic monster.

As the stories unwind, we see how they have merged and
mixed over the years and how allegory has finally replaced
myth and history.

BIBLIOGRAPHY

Bérenger-Féraud, L. J. B. *Réminiscences populaires de la Provence.* Paris: Ernest Leroux, 1885.

La Légende Dorée (written about 1255 by L'Abbé J.-B.M.
Roze). Edition in French by Jacques de Voragine, vol. 2.
Paris: Edouard Rouveyre, 1902.

Guide de la Provence mystérieuse, Les Guides Noirs. Paris:
Tchou, 1965.

The Evil Weed

THE LADY OF THE MOOR

The moors of the Val-de-Saire are quite unusual in summer. Then flowers like yellow butterflies, dwarfed green gorse, ash-gray heather with scarlet blooms, common heather with pale rose tufts—all grow at nearly the same height, making elaborate patterns like those of an oriental rug. But in the winter, the wind from the sea whips the tawny leaves from the young beech trees, and the carpet loses its color, leaving only the bare sandy moor with a few short grasses and weeds.

On such a day, young Gaston Bianchon returned alone on horseback to Normandy where he was born. His family had left the Val-de-Saire when he was only an infant and had moved to the inland province of Bourbonnais. Gaston had never seen the sea. Now, his father having died and left him his horse, Gaston was coming to the end of his long journey to the town of Barfleur where he would stay with his old aunt.

Beyond the moor he could see the sea and he wished to hurry to it. Besides, he had grown hungry and the strong wind whirling around him seemed to make his hunger more intense. And so, instead of continuing along the main road, he took a side road toward the harbor town of St. Vaast, which he could see below him, and where he thought he might find a tavern and some food. The town was farther along the road than it looked from above, but it did not matter. He had been on this trip a good many days and a few extra kilometers were of no importance. This had been a lucky journey and his luck held. In a short while he saw an old gentleman and a small boy standing in front of a cottage and he stopped to ask directions.

"You need go no farther," said the old gentleman. "Stop with us, and my grandson and I will find you a crust or two."

The offer pleased Gaston, and the young boy, Pierre, showed him where he could pasture his horse in a nearby field. Then they both returned to the cottage where the grandfather had set out some fresh bread, some cheese, and some cider.

"So you are on your way to Barfleur," said the grandfather as he cut the bread into large chunks.

"I am," replied Gaston. "It is sixteen years since I was born there and my father has told me so many fine stories about it that I have been impatient to return."

"Did your father tell you about the Evil Weed and the Lady who haunts the moor?" asked Pierre.

Gaston laughed. "He did! And one scarcely has heard a wilder tale than that one."

The grandfather frowned. "Would you laugh, too, if I told you that my own father, rest his soul, had seen the Lady with his own eyes?"

"With respect to your father, sir, I would still laugh."

"Laugh away, then! But let me tell you, if you were to walk there in the day, I admit you would see nothing unusual—just flowers and weeds growing tightly together in summer, a few weeds and grasses now, a few beech trees, and in the distance, the sea."

"I was on such a moor on my way here," said Gaston.

"And I'll wager you did not notice the Evil Weed."

Gaston gulped his cider. "No, you are right. I did not notice the Evil Weed."

"And neither has anyone," the grandfather said, "though they know the paths of the moor by heart. And that is because it changes its shape and its color, and it creeps among the gorse at night to confuse and mislead the traveler. I could tell you about men who have known the moor since they were children, yet have lost their way because of the Evil Weed."

"And still, I thought you said it was a lady who haunted the moor," said Gaston.

"They are the same," said the grandfather.

"The Lady and the weed are the same. Come now!"

"It is the truth. She has become part of the moor—an evil

part. It is even known who the Lady is. She belonged to an old family, well known in these parts. But she was a tyrant, that one—hard with the servants, impatient with everyone, vengeful, not to mention greedy.

"Then, one time there was a quarrel between her parish of Valcanville and the next parish of Montfarville. The matter was about the moor. Both claimed it. Then this lady grew quite furious at all the arguments and she stamped her foot and swore, 'If after my death I had one foot in heaven and one foot in hell, I would take out the first one in order to have the whole moor.' "

"And that was blasphemy," said young Pierre, who had been listening and nodding his head. He had heard the story many times, but he could hear it again and again.

"She never married," the grandfather continued. "And she got on with no one. Finally she fell very ill, but she wanted no priest, though he had often begged her to make peace with her enemies, and above all to take back her evil threat about the moor. She would have none of it. She died unforgiving and unforgiven."

There was no sound in the room now except the rising of the wind and a slapping of small branches across the windows.

"A strange thing happened after that," the old man said. "When her coffin was to be taken from the courtyard onto a cart for burial, no one could lift it. They harnessed six horses to it, but it would not budge. There was nothing to do but dig the grave under it right there. They put stones above it and the stone became part of the courtyard of the manor. You can see it for yourself if you want to."

"Now you think that's the end of the story, don't you?" asked Pierre. "Grandfather, tell him . . ."

"Right after that," the grandfather said, "a man was walking home across the moor from Valcanville to Montfarville—and he knew the way so well he could have done it backward with his hands over his eyes—and he lost his way. Round and round he went across the moor, returning to the same spot, over and over, seeing the same trees, the same rocks, and all the time he was led by the laughing voice of a woman . . . leading him deeper into the moor."

"Ah, that is a very good tale," said Gaston.

"A story, yes; a tale, no," said the grandfather. "I'll tell you there was not a more truthful man than my own son, this boy's father," he patted Pierre on the head "—now dead, rest his soul—and he had something happen to him on the moor. He was coming by horseback from Cherbourg where he had been having a little celebration with some friends, so he was late coming home. And as he was riding the road along the moor, he heard a sweet voice say, 'Oh, where can I stay the night?' My son, a pleasant man, said, 'Oh, hop on my horse

with me!' And suddenly the Lady appeared. And there was
no doubt it was she—he saw her clearly. As she jumped into
the saddle the horse started to whinny and rear and then took
off at a gallop. My son turned in the saddle and saw she was
dressed all in flowing white and that her teeth had become
very long. And while he looked at her she disappeared.

"When the horse stopped, my son found they had been
driven right into the pond, and he said that the horse then
took off so fast it was as if he had a fire behind him."

"Please do not think me disrespectful," young Gaston
said. "I am sure your son was a truthful man. And my father
was truthful and told me stories, too, though not so many as
you have. He said that a priest nearly perished on the moor
one very cold night when he was only a few hundred feet
from his home. But my great-uncle heard his cries in the
morning and helped him. He was tangled in vines. He said
he had thought someone was lost on the moor and he went to
see. In the end, it was he who was lost. But priests, too, can
take a bit too much wine, can they not? And perhaps your
son?"

"I can see you are still in doubt," said the grandfather.
"Well, then ask anyone about a weaver named Jean Paulet.
He was coming back from town with a big package of thread
on the end of his walking stick. And then he heard a voice
calling him. 'Jean Paulet! Jean Paulet!' So he left the road

and he walked in the direction of the voice, but it kept moving. Then he began stumbling all over the moor, falling over those wretched mounds of earth, tangling in weeds, his thread bobbing around on the end of his walking stick. And every time he stopped the voice would call again in the night . . ."

"Jean Paulet! Jean Paulet!" Pierre did the calling this time.

The grandfather took a sip of cider to wet his throat. "Ah, well! Finally he went mad and ran about the moor yelling, 'What do you want of me, damned spirit?' And that is how they found him next morning, running round and round, screaming at the Lady, who was not to be seen nor heard by then. But she had not left poor Jean. He would not walk that road again, ever. He gave up his trade and he just sat and talked to people—mostly the children because they liked to listen—and he would tell them about that night when he followed the Lady's voice and got tangled in the Evil Weed. And sometimes when he was talking he would suddenly stop and cry, 'What do you want of me?' Just like that."

"Why does it not occur to anyone that it could have been the wind?" asked Gaston. "After all, this Jean did not see the Lady. He did not see anything at all."

"Does the wind make you lose your way?" asked Pierre.

"It could blow you off the path, surely," replied Gaston.

"Oh yes, it could do that if it were a strong enough wind," the grandfather agreed. "But have you ever been blown so far off a path that you could not find your way back to it?"

"No, and I have never walked in an Evil Weed, nor heard a strange lady call me over the moor, and I don't expect to either. But we have been talking so long and I have stayed too late. It will be midnight before I reach my aunt's house." And Gaston rose to leave, thanking them for the fine meal and good talk. Young Pierre ran to fetch the horse from the pasture and Gaston let him ride the horse up the road a way before they said good-by.

Feeling a bit full, Gaston decided to walk awhile, and so he led his horse up the rather steep hill and along the side roads that led out of the town. He did not hurry and he sang as he went, feeling well and cheerful after his supper and cider and the amusing stories. And so darkness fell before he had expected and before he had reached the main road. However, he was not worried. He had been told that it was easy to find his aunt's home, just follow the main road and when he arrived at Barfleur, it would be the second house on the right as one descended the hill.

Gaston found the main road with no trouble, mounted his horse and headed in a straight line for Barfleur. He had been riding for perhaps an hour when suddenly he heard a wailing sound. He thought it was the wind and continued on his

way. When he heard it a second time, he thought that it was
not the wind so much as his imagination. But the third time
he was sure that it was neither. A voice was calling his name,
calling it plaintively and urgently. "Gaston Bianchon! Gaston Bianchon!"

"Ah," he thought to himself, "I must be nearing my
aunt's house and perhaps she has sent someone out to look for
me."

"Halloo," he called. "This is Gaston, over here."

"Gaston Bianchon," called the voice, and it was that of a
woman.

"My aunt, herself," thought Gaston. And he called, "Here
I am, Aunt. I'm coming." And he turned toward the sound
of the voice, calling, "Wait a minute, Aunt. I'm over here."

"Gaston Bianchon!" cried the voice, and it seemed to come
from another direction.

Gaston turned his horse and headed across the moor, calling again, "Here I am. This is Gaston, over here."

And then, in the darkness of the moor, he caught sight of
something light moving quickly. It seemed to be a figure in
a flowing white garment, and as his horse overtook the running figure Gaston reached out to stop her, but all he caught
was a piece of her dress. And as she turned and looked over
her shoulder, he saw her very long teeth and over-bright
eyes.

"On the head of my father!" Gaston exclaimed. "I swear I

am seeing the Lady of the moor, for that is not my aunt. I am told she is short and stout." And as he said this, the Lady disappeared and Gaston, still grasping a scrap of her dress, found himself deep in the moor, far from the road, and with no idea in what direction to go. Round and round he went, and when he and the horse were both exhausted they stopped near a big boulder that they had passed many times in their mad chase. But before he slept Gaston put the scrap of dress in his shirt pocket for safekeeping.

He slept deeply during the night, but when dawn broke he awoke quite weary nevertheless. He looked across the moor, now hung with fog, and shivered. But taking his direction from the shrouded sun, he found the road and resumed his journey to Barfleur.

"Little Gaston!" cried his aunt when she saw him. "Gaston Bianchon! How glad I am to see you!" And when she said his name, Gaston remembered the experience of the night before and he told his aunt about it.

"Oh, Nephew!" said his aunt. "I've heard that story all my life from many men who stay out late, but even now it is hard to believe."

"I, myself, did not believe it," said Gaston. "But we will both have to believe it this time because I have caught a piece of the Lady's dress and I have it in my pocket to show you."

"Have you, indeed!" said the aunt. "Well, that will be something, at least. Let's see it then."

Gaston then emptied the contents of his shirt pocket into his hand. It lay in his palm, the evidence of what he had seen—*a sprig of a plant that was not familiar to him.*

"A piece of her dress!" cried the aunt. "Why that's nothing but some kind of weed."

"Yes," Gaston said with more wonder than fear. "Yes. It *is* some kind of weed!"

A FEW WORDS ABOUT THE STORY OF
THE EVIL WEED

In local legend, the lady of the moor may be a green lady or a white lady, and she may be linked with the evil weed or she may not be. The writer, Thuriet, in his nineteenth-century collection of folktales, tells about the green lady of Thise who transformed herself into a black goat and led many a greedy farmer into dangerous predicaments. The goat would appear several yards from the farmer, but when he moved to seize her the goat would jump away. The farmer would approach stealthily, but the goat would elude him. And it continued this way until the goat had led the man into a muddy hole in the ground.

It is said that almost any marsh or moor of significant size has its green or white lady, but only some fields and woods have an evil weed. It may be called *la male herbe* (the evil weed), in Normandy, or *l'herbe qui égare* (the grass that leads you astray), in Franche-Comté, or *landrine* (of the sandy moor) from the area of Toulouse in southwest France.

To believe in the existence of such a weed is frightening and yet convenient, too. It might excuse many otherwise unexplained delays or absences and very likely keeps some children from straying too far from home after nightfall.

BIBLIOGRAPHY

Fleury, Jean. *Littérature orale de la Basse Normandie* (*Hague et Val-de-Saire*). Paris: Maisonneuve & Cie., 1883.

Thuriet, Ch. *Traditions populaires du Doubs.* Paris: Emile Lechevalier, 1891.

Thε VOUIVRε

THE FLYING SERPENT

All year round, the serpent called the Vouivre guarded a treasure of gold and silver in a cave high on a rocky crag. But once a year at midnight of the Sunday before Easter when the people were in church, the Vouivre left her aerie and flew to the clear spring near Bourg to drink and to wash her sparkling wings. That was when the door of the treasure cave swung wide open, and for just those few minutes the gold and silver on that high cliff was left unguarded. Through the years many people had tried to steal it, but at the last word of the church service, when the bell began to toll, the door swung shut, the Vouivre returned, and woe be to anyone who was inside the cave then.

When not in her hole near the cave or on the ledge in front of it, the Vouivre might be seen flying, circling the rock, always in sight of the treasure, though her vision was wide and far-seeing. Then she was an awesome sight, with her enormous, shining green wings on her great serpent's body, covered with sonorous scales which gave off a low and strange musical sound as she flew. She wore a crown of pearls and a gold circlet on her tail which rang. But most strange of all was her dragon's head with its one great and glowing ruby eye. This luminous orb she removed when she bathed, mak-

73

ing herself blind for just those minutes. At night she could be seen from afar, the ruby eye blazing in the dark, its red glow acting as her lantern, so bright that she seemed to be on fire.

It was well known that if, by chance, someone could reach the cave while the Vouivre was bathing and if that person were to cast a piece of stale bread inside, everything that the crumbs of the bread touched would belong to him. And then if he could take the treasure and cross a stream of water with it, the Vouivre would be unable to get it back. Some had done just that, staying away from the midnight service, waiting for the Vouivre to leave the cave, and then creeping up the rock and into the cave and stuffing their pockets and sacks with gold. But some had taken so much they could hardly move. They had been quickly overtaken and cruelly scarred by the Vouivre's burning eye. One man had reached the stream and crossed it and hidden his treasure well. But two days later he had died of a mysterious ailment and the gold that he had found and hidden was never found again.

Once, many years ago, there was a man named Roger Christophe who, with his wife Louise and their young son Claude, lived in a small cottage on a little farm near Bourg. They were quite poor but they did not think that any disgrace and were as happy as if they were lords of a manor. But there came a time when the price of the wheat that they grew

brought very little money and they had only a few sous a day
with which to buy food. Still, they had the pig and the white
goat and they tried to get along. But soon it was necessary to
sell the pig, and after that the goat. And even that money
did not last long and they were always hungry. Roger gave
all the food to Louise and Claude and he searched in the
woods for wild roots and the fruit of the beech tree for himself. But this was not enough and he became very weak. One
day he became ill and Louise brought him some herb soup.
But Roger said, "No, I have eaten today. Truly I have. You
and Claude must drink that."

Early in the year Roger died and Louise mourned deeply.
She worked very hard to feed young Claude and the neighbors tried to help her, but she remained sad and lonely.

And then one evening—it was on the eve of Palm
Sunday—Louise was dozing in her chair by the fire after put-
ting young Claude to bed. And while she napped, she had a
dream. In it she saw a beautiful woman seated on the rock of
the Vouivre and the woman was beckoning and pointing
with her finger at the open cave filled with gold and silver.
Louise saw it all clearly. She awoke and said, "The dream
means that I am to go there." So she arose and, taking young
Claude in her arms, she took the path out of the town,
crossed the stream, and began the steep climb to the great
rock on the mountain. It could be seen clearly above her in

the moonlight, its great ledge lit by the fiery red eye of the Vouivre.

Claude, now fully awake, asked, "Why can't I walk, too, Mama?"

But Louise answered, "Your legs are too short for this climb and we must hurry to get to the ledge by midnight." And so she carried Claude the whole way. They arrived at a grassy knoll just below the cave sometime before midnight, and Louise took Claude into the shadow of the crag, waiting for the serpent to leave.

"Why must we stay here?" Claude asked.

"Shhhh . . ." whispered Louise. "We must be very quiet so as not to anger the Vouivre. But when we go up to the ledge, you may throw this crust into the cave and anything the crumbs touch will be ours." And then she gave Claude the little crust of bread she had brought with her.

Louise was very tired from the climb but she kept her eyes open and waited. There was no sound but the gusting of the wind, the calling of an owl, and the beating of Louise's heart. The red glow of the Vouivre's eye cast an eerie glow over the rocks. But at midnight there was a clear sound—the tolling of the church bell for the midnight service. Above them, the Vouivre spread her great green wings, shining in the light of her own bright lantern, and her scales added the sound of castanets to the ringing of the bell as she flew off for her yearly drink and bath at the spring.

The moment the Vouivre left the ledge, Louise took Claude in her arms and climbed the rest of the way to the crag, the moon lighting her path, and as she reached the ledge of the Vouivre the moon showed the way straight through the opened rock door into the cave. They had reached the rock at the last stroke of the church bell and so Louise fell to her knees and began to pray. But young Claude ran ahead through the open doorway, casting the crust of bread before him and sitting down to play with the gold that lined the cave. Louise's fatigue had overcome her, and when she closed her eyes in prayer she fell into a light sleep. As she slept, Claude stacked the shining coins to build a great tower, and when it fell from its own weight he made lovely patterns with them on the rocky floor.

In the town below the last words of the service were said and the bell began to toll again. The sound awoke Louise. Too late! The Vouivre was winging her way back to the crag, the rocky door had closed with young Claude inside, and the cave would not be open again for another year.

Louise beat upon the door and cried, "Claude! Claude!" but it was no use. Now, the Vouivre's red glow was close and Louise fled in terror and despair to the place below, where she and Claude had hidden earlier. There she wept until daylight when she fell asleep from exhaustion.

When Louise had not returned all day, the people of the town set out to look for her. They found her that afternoon,

crumpled and still weeping. They heard her story in horror
and begged her to return home, but she would not move
from the spot. A storm was blowing up and so they built a
shelter over her with branches and leaves, and sadly they left
her there.

All night the wind screamed around the rock of the
Vouivre and the rain beat against the cliff, but Louise did not
notice it. She thought only of her child locked in the serpent's treasure cave, and she prayed and she wept. The next
day neighbors came again bringing the priest with them, but
even he could not persuade her to leave. They had brought
her some bread and a bowl of milk. She took a bite of the
bread and a sip of the milk and then, while the Vouivre was
circling the rock on her evening flight, Louise climbed to the
ledge and put the rest of the bread and the milk in front of
the cave. Then she returned to her shelter.

The same thing happened the next day. The people from
the village came and brought Louise milk and bread with a
bit of honey. She took a bite of the bread and a sip of the
milk, and later she took them and put them before the door
of the cave. There she found that yesterday's bowl was empty
and the bread was gone.

Then Louise knew what she would do. She made her
shelter more secure against the strong wind and wove a mat
of grasses to cover the rock on which she slept. This became
her home. Each day she accepted the milk and bread that one

of the villagers brought her, but she took only a bite and a
sip and carried the rest to the cave. And though she kept
busy finding berries and mushrooms and the fruit of the
beech tree for herself, she prayed many hours for the welfare
of her son and she cried often—so much that her tears filled a
hollow in the rock.

A year passed this way. And then, on the night before
Palm Sunday, Louise dreamed again of the lady pointing to
the open door of the rock, and in her dream she tried to see
within but she could see nothing. She awoke feeling anxious
and afraid as the church bell began to toll for the midnight
service. Just as it happened the year before, at the sound of
the bell the Vouivre spread her great green wings and, lit by
her ruby eye, flew from the cliff, out over the woods and
toward the spring to drink and bathe.

Louise sprang from her shelter beneath the ledge and
climbed quickly up to the rock of the Vouivre. The door now
stood open, and Louise, stopping for nothing, ran into the
cave. She did not even notice the riches at her feet, but
looked about trying to adapt her eyesight to the cave, lit only
by moonlight falling on gold.

"Claude!" she called, weeping. "Claude!" And she looked
everywhere. And then in a corner she saw a sort of bundle.
She ran to the corner and touched the bundle gently. It
moved and turned, and then the child opened his eyes.

"Mama!" he cried and embraced her. Louise, too thankful

to talk, only wept and held him close, cradling him in her arms.

But time was passing and Louise suddenly leaped up and, holding Claude closely under her cape, she ran from the cave and down the rocky path, looking over her shoulder from time to time in fear that the Vouivre would pursue her in anger. She crossed the stream just as the first sound of the church bell announced the end of the service, and arrived in the village square as the townspeople were coming from church.

The priest himself now came out of the church and saw her. "Louise," he called to her through the darkened square. "Is that you?" And he came closer and looked at her face. "And you look so full of joy. Have you found the treasure?"

"Yes," said Louise, uncovering young Claude. "Here it is!"

"I have a treasure, too," said Claude, and he put his hand in his pocket and held up one big goldpiece.

It is said that tracings of the Vouivre's scales are still marked on those rocks, and that the pool Louise made with her tears is never empty. It is told, too, that after many years an enchanted flutist finally lured the Vouivre into an oven that had been made especially to burn her. But some people say that she escaped death because of her magical powers. Whatever is true, she comes no more to the rock.

A FEW WORDS ABOUT THE STORY OF
THE VOUIVRE

Whether she is called the *vouivre* (pronounced vweevre), or *wivre,* or *guibre,* she is the same winged serpent of fire who for centuries terrified the people of France. She was most often seen in Franche-Comté, a region bordering Switzerland, as well as in the more centrally located regions of Nivernais, Bourbonnais, and Burgundy. People could argue late into the night about her appearance. Some said her eye was a diamond, and others were sure it was a ruby. Some said her crown was of diamonds, while others said it was of pearls. Some were sure she was beautiful, and others just as sure that she was ugly. But the fact of her existence was not questioned.

The stories of all regions generally agree that once or twice a year, on the eve of Christmas or Easter, the *vouivre* would leave her treasure to bathe and quench her thirst at the local fountain, river, or pond, leaving her eye on the bank. Then, and only for those few minutes while the *vouivre* was blind and vulnerable, could her hidden treasure be plundered or her jeweled eye and crown be stolen.

There are many stories of how the *vouivre* was caught, or of attempts to catch her. Several of them have to do with a washtub or barrel stuck full of spikes. The idea was for the would-be conqueror to stand behind the barrel to lure the serpent. But when she leaped at him, he would jump under the barrel just in time, and the *vouivre* would be stuck on the spikes. Sometimes this worked, but more often the *vouivre* was free again to light up the night with her glowing eye.

BIBLIOGRAPHY

Beauquier, Ch. *Faune et flore populaires de la Franche-Comté,* vol. 1. Paris: Ernest Leroux, 1910.

Clément-Janin, M. H., ed. *Traditions populaires de la Côte d'Or.* Dijon: 1884.

Desforges, A. "Vieilles légendes du Nivernais (La Pierre de la Wivre du Beuvray et la pauvre Jeanne)," from PARIS-CENTRE, Nevers, 23 Dec. 1941.

Drouillet, Jean. *Folklore du Nivernais et du Morvan.* La Charité sur Loire: M. Bernadat, 1964.

Monnier, D., and Vingtrinier, M. E. A. *Croyances et traditions populaires recueillies dans la Franche-Comté, le Lyonnais, la Bresse, et le Bugey.* Lyon: Henri Georg, 1874.

About the Authors

FELICE HOLMAN is the author of many distinguished books for young people, among which are—*Slake's Limbo,* which was selected as an ALA Notable book for young adults and children, *The Escape of the Giant Hogstalk, I Hear You Smiling, The Cricket Winter* and *The Future of Hooper Toote.* She lives in Westport, Connecticut.

NANINE VALEN received her B.A. from Bryn Mawr College and has done graduate work at Yale University. She has lived in the south of France, where she made a study of the folklore. She is presently working in children's television in New York City.